To my Grandmother,
who is always on the go, but definitely isn't a dinosaur!
(I promised you a frog book, but since your tastes have changed
I hope this will do.)

—Love your Granddaughter, K.W.

For the Turlingtons—Ellen, Lew, Roger, and Leonie—
who are always "on the go!"

—With love, L.R.

With thanks to David Eng-Wong and his son John Liam for the inspiration!

Little, Brown and Company

Time Warner Book Group
1271 Avenue of the Americas, New York, NY, 10020
Visit our Web site at www.lb-kids.com

First Edition

        Library of Congress Cataloging-in-Publication Data

Wilson, Karma.
    Dinos on the go / by Karma Wilson ; illustrated by Laura Rader.—lst ed.
        p. cm.
    Summary: Dinosaurs ride everything from bicycles to airplanes as they travel around the world.
    ISBN 0-316-73811-5
    [1. Dinosaurs—Fiction. 2. Travel—Fiction. 3. Stories in rhyme.] I. Rader, Laura, ill. II.
    Title.

    PZ8.3.W6976Di 2003   2003047485
    [E]—dc21

10 9 8 7 6 5 4 3 2 1

Book design by Saho Fujii

TWP

Printed in Singapore

The illustrations for this book were done in Acrylics and ink on Strathmore bristol paper.
The text was set in Newboyd, and the display type was hand-lettered by Laura Rader.

DINOS ON THE GO!

by KARMA WILSON

Illustrated by LAURA RADER

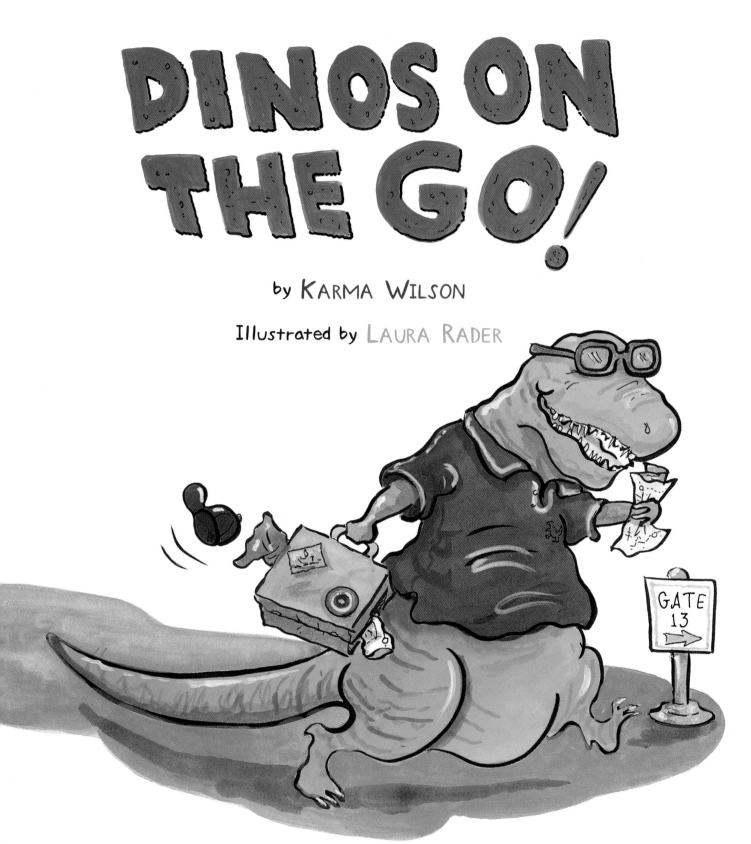

 LITTLE, BROWN AND COMPANY

New York ⁓ Boston

To visit Spain,
Portland, Maine,
or maybe Timbuktu?

Dinos, dinos, on the go.
How will they travel there?

In trucks and trains
and jet airplanes.

Look out! They're everywhere.

Triceratops is tearing through
the town in his old truck.
The way he's swerving here and there—
it seems he's run amuck!

Dinos on the go . . .
Clear the way!

BEEP, BEEP!

Dryosaurus drives his dragster.
Boy, he sure is fast!
Officials wave the checkered flag
as he goes speeding past.

Dinos on the go . . .

Clear the way!

VROOM, VROOM!

Barosaurus rides her bike
along the boulevard.
She waves at everyone she sees.
They're staring mighty hard.

Dinos, dinos, on the go.
Why are they on the run?

They're on their way
to meet and play
and have some dino-fun!

Come see us!
Love, Aunt
Milly
and Uncle Willy

REPTILE
RETREAT

OLD FOSSIL
FALLS

Dinos, dinos, on the go.
Whom will they go to see?
Old Aunt Milly,
Uncle Willy,
friends and family!

CARNOSAUR CREEK

Greetings! from Snow Dome

MAMMOTH MOUNTAINS

Saurusville

FOOD, GAS and more FOOD!

CLAWTOOTH CANYON

JAWBONE

Stegosaurus sails her ship
across the seven seas.
She's rushing through the rolling waves.
There's really quite a breeze.

Dinos on the go . . .
Clear the way!
CLANG, CLANG!

T. rex takes his family out
to travel on the train.
The sleeping cars are slightly small.
Let's hope they don't complain!

Dinos on the go . . .
Clear the way!

CHOO, CHOO!

Anxious Allosaurus rides
an airplane in the sky.
She doesn't want a window seat.
The plane is mighty high!

Dinos on the go . . .
Clear the way!

ZOOM, ZOOM!

Not today.
They're on their way.
Those dinos love to roam!

Dinos, dinos, finally there.
They've reached their goal at last.

The party's on!
They'll dance till dawn
and have a dino-blast!